Inspired by my wonderful children

By Christine Butler-Jones

Johnny has an AMAZING imagination. He sometimes imagines he's a superhero defeating a giant bear!

"Stay back you wild beast"

He also likes to imagine he is king of all of
Toy Land!

"I am in charge here"

Whilst he is king of all the toys, he orders his digger to carry all his cars back to his toy box.

"That way please"

He orders his soldiers to line up nearly ready for battle!

"ATTENTION!! Ready, March"

He orders his rocket to take him to Mars so he can explore!

When his rocket arrives on mars, Johnny meets some friendly aliens who show him around their planet.

Johnny likes it on Mars.

Back home on Earth, Johnny also likes to imagine he's a world class footballer who is scoring goals for his country!

Everyone cheers for Johnny!

"Hooray!!"

At bath time, Johnny imagines he's a Pirate stealing treasures from lost ships under the sea!

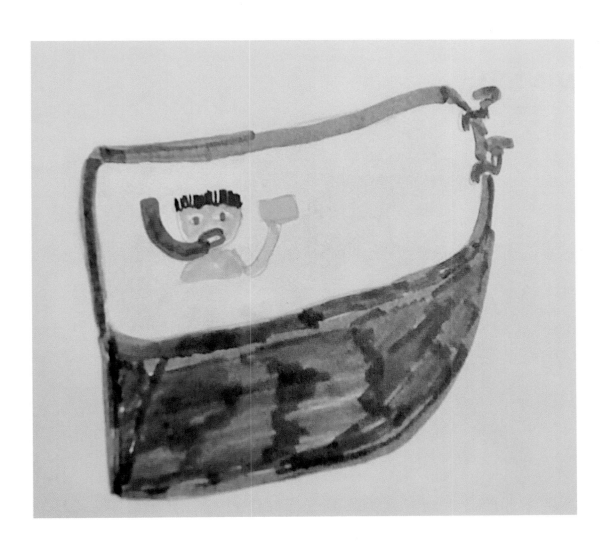

Sometimes he imagines he's a racer in a very fast car zooming to the finish line!

"WINNER"

At dinner time Johnny sneaks some broccoli off of his plate so he can imagine he's a giant stomping high above the trees!

"STOMP STOMP"

Johnny has lots of fun with his imagination, but sometimes Johnny's imagination can scare him.

He imagines there's a troll hiding under his bed waiting for him to fall asleep!

He imagines there's a beast hiding in his cupboard, ready to pounce when he walks by.

Or maybe a monster peeping from behind the curtains.

He sometimes imagines there's a huge spider hovering above his head ready to wrap him in its web and then gobble him up!

This is very scary for Johnny and sometimes means he can not sleep or is scared to go to bed.

Johnnys brother Paul reminds him one night that he has an amazing imagination and this is actually a real super power, because in his imagination he can make ANYTHING happen however he chooses.

So, even if he imagines something scary like a beast hiding in his cupboard, or peeping from behind his curtains, or if imagining a troll hiding under the bed, he can also imagine a way to make them go away.

Johnny is excited by this realisation and puts his imagination to work straight away!

He Imagines a magnetic field around his bed which prevents any beast or troll from coming near whilst he sleeps, by zapping them if they dare try!

"Zap zap"

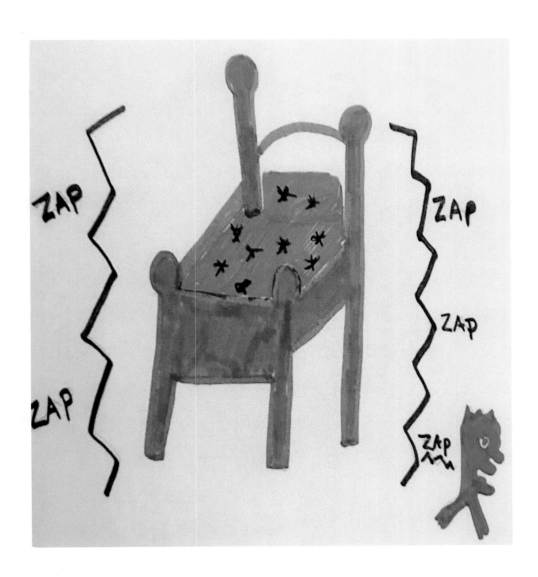

He imagines he has a magic blanket with infra red lasers that destroy any beast who dares to enter his room!

He imagines his cupboard had a secret magic password that only he knows, nothing can get inside without the code.

"What's the code?"

Johnny imagines he is totally invisible, with a click of his fingers nothing can see him!

"Click"

Johnny is in charge of his imagination, even the scary ones.

Johnny can now sleep soundly at night without being scared, using all the ideas in his amazing imagination.

What can you imagine with your amazing imagination?

Johnny gets a
VACCINATION

Christine Butler

Johnny and his sister Shannon are due for a vaccination on Friday and Johnny is feeling very worried.

"Will it hurt?" He asks Shannon

"I don't think it will hurt much Johnny" says Shannon.

"Let's not worry about it now anyway, we're going to the park and it's going to be great fun! There's no point in letting it ruin all the fun today is there?" She continued

At the park Shannon is excited as she spins around and around on the roundabout. "Come on Johnny" she calls excitedly. But Johnny Is worrying about his vaccination, he can't possibly enjoy himself on the roundabout or anything else.

"What if the needle makes me bleed all over the floor" he wonders.

When Johnny and Shannon get back home, Dad puts on a movie and mum brings some treats for them to enjoy whilst watching.

This is Johnnys favourite movie, but he's not able to watch and he can't enjoy eating any treats, his tummy feels funny.

Johnny is worrying about his vaccination.

"Is it a big needle?" He asks, "I don't think so Johnny and it's not happening today anyway, let's watch the movie" Shannon replies.

Johnny starts feeling a little sick.

Later on at bath time Shannon is having lots of fun splashing around and pretending to be a shark under the sea.

Johnny can't enjoy his bath at all, Johnny is worrying about his vaccination.

"Will it bleed?" He asks.

"Maybe a little but not much" replies Shannon "and it's not happening today anyway so try not to worry Johnny.

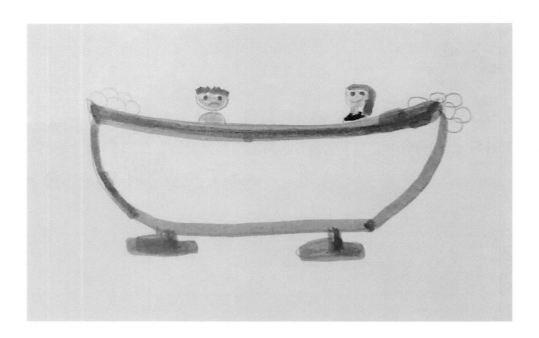

It's time for bed and Shannon quickly falls to sleep with happy thoughts about her fun day.

Johnny can't sleep, he is still worrying about his vaccination.

Morning arrives and it's time to get ready to go to school, Johnny is tired and is feeling sick and doesn't want to go to school.

Mum tells Johnny to go back to bed "maybe you have a tummy bug" she says

But Johnny is not sick, he is worrying about his vaccination "does it take long?" He asks Shannon before she leaves

"No it should be very quick" she replies before skipping off to school. "Get some rest Johnny " says Mum.

Johnny goes back to bed but he quickly wakes after a bad dream, he had a horrible dream that his arm fell off when the needle went in!

Poor Johnny is so worried about his vaccination

Johnny starts to cry "I don't want a vaccination!!" He cries out.

Dad hears Johnny cry and comes to see what's happening. "What's wrong Johnny?" He asks

"I'm scared of having my vaccination" he says

"Now now Johnny, what's worrying you so much about a vaccination?" Dad asks

"I'm scared of the big needle, I'm scared it will be big and sharp and will hurt a lot"

"I'm scared there will be lots of blood"

Johnny is very very upset.

"That sounds like a lot of worries Johnny"
says Dad

"There's no need to worry so much, it's just a small needle and you will only feel a tiny pinch, there definitely won't be blood everywhere I promise you"

"Please try not to worry Johnny, everything will be ok".

Dad gives Johnny a hug and he starts to calm down.

Johnny feels much better talking to Dad about his worries, talking about worries will always help, even if it's just a little.

Johnny hears a knock at the door, Shannon is home from school, he runs to see her.

"You missed a great day at school today Johnny, Mr Smith stood on a skateboard by mistake and flew straight into the goal, everyone saw it happen, it was so funny! Even Mr smith laughed himself".

"How are you feeling now Johnny? Are you still feeling sick?" She asks.

Johnny is feeling a lot better than before, especially after hearing about Mr Smith skateboarding into the goal!

"I wish I had been there" he giggles

"I'm feeling much better now, but I'm still worried about our vaccination, are you not worried Shannon ? Even a little?" He asks

" Not really Johnny" she replies " it's not happening today and I prefer to wait until the time comes"

Shannon continues to tell Johnny about a time when she was worried…..

"It was my first visit to the dentist" she started "and just like you Johnny I was very worried, I worried for 3 whole days about what MIGHT happen, I asked lots of questions but I still worried! I even missed Laura's Birthday party,

"When the time came for my dentist appointment, it wasn't scary at all. I was worried all that time for nothing,

So now" she continued "if something worries me and I have already spoken to an adult about my worries, I put my worry on the worry shelf in my mind and wait until the time comes to see for myself" our imaginations can be very scary otherwise".

Johnny finds this idea very interesting and decides he too will try to put his worry about his vaccination on the worry shelf.

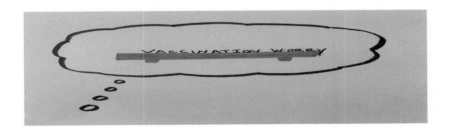

Johnny and Shannon wrap up warm and go out to play in the park for a while.

This time they BOTH enjoy spinning around and around on the roundabout and they both enjoy running around playing chase.

They both have a great time!

When they arrive back home, Johnny enjoys a nice warm cup of hot chocolate.

Johnnys worries are on the worry shelf.

The day arrives and it's time for Johnny and Shannon to get their vaccination.

On the way to the nurses office, both Johnny and Shannon start to feel a little worried. It's ok to feel worried when we are about to do something and we don't know exactly what's going to happen.

When they arrive, the kind nurse reassures them both and explains "it will just be a quick pinch" she also explains what the vaccination is for.

"Vaccines are super important, they make our bodies very strong! They encourage our bodies to make antibodies against a disease, antibodies are like soldiers who fight off the disease when we come into contact with it and this means it can't make us sick".

"Wow" says Johnny "that sounds so cool"

"It is" says the nurse with a smile.

Johnny is first to get his vaccination and is super surprised at how quick it happened and he barely felt a thing.

Shannon is next and is also surprised at how quickly it's over "it really is just a small pinch" she says

"Now we have super soldiers to stop us getting sick" says Johnny proudly.

Johnny didn't need to worry after all and he didn't need to miss out on all the fun.

Most things are scarier in our imaginations than in real life because when we think "what if" our super brains can think up lots of things that can be scary.

If you are worrying about something, always speak to an adult who can help and reassure you and if you are still worrying, try your own "worry shelf" and wait until the time comes. You might be pleasantly surprised just like Johnny.

Johnny is feeling ANGRY

BY CHRISTINE BUTLER

Johnny can sometimes get angry.

Anger is an emotion that we can feel if we believe we are being treated unfairly or if we see someone else is being treated unfairly.

Anger is a very normal emotion and can be helpful if used in the right ways.
It gives us a reason to stand up for ourselves or if we believe someone else is being treated unfairly, our anger emotion will give us a reason to speak up against this treatment.

It will also give us a reason to stand up for things we believe in.

But sometimes we can feel angry and our reactions to the anger can cause problems.

Anger that is out of control can be very harmful to ourselves and others around us.

One day Johnny is sent to his room for time out as he refuses to play fairly with his brother and sisters.

When Johnny gets to his room he is feeling so angry that he kicks his toy truck, he kicks it with such fury that the truck flies into the air and straight towards his fish tank that is sitting on his desk.

As the truck hits the glass on the fish tank it comes crashing down, glass and water everywhere, the poor little fish are left flapping on his desk.

Johnnys mum comes rushing to his room, she checks Johnny hasn't been injured, then she rescues his goldfish by quickly putting them in a bowl of water whilst she gets to cleaning up the dangerous mess.

Johnny didn't mean for this to happen, he has allowed his anger emotion to control him.

This has led to dangerous and disastrous consequences. Johnny is now feeling very sad about what he has done.

"You must learn to control your anger Johnny!" Says mum.

It's bath time and Johnny seems to have forgotten all about his poor fish and his fish tank, he's having lots of fun splashing around playing with his toy submarine and his toy shark.

Johnny is imagining his shark is trying to get into the submarine to eat the submariners, submariners are the people who go down under the sea in a submarine.

Johnny has been in the bath for a long time and it is now time for him to get out, but Johnny doesn't want to get out, even though he has started to turn into a sponge.

Mum takes the plug out and the water starts to drain away, Johnny is feeling angry again! He is feeling so angry, that he starts to shout at his mum.

"You're the worst mum EVER! You ruin everything and I HATE you" says Johnny.

Poor Mum is feeling very sad and hurt by this outburst.

Johnny is now feeling very guilty about what he said to his mum, he didn't mean what he said, he didn't want to hurt his mums feelings but it's too late! He has spoken in anger.

Johnny has allowed his anger emotion to control him again.

It's Johnnys bedtime and Johnny lies awake thinking about what he said to his mum "I hope she knows I didn't mean it" he thinks to himself.

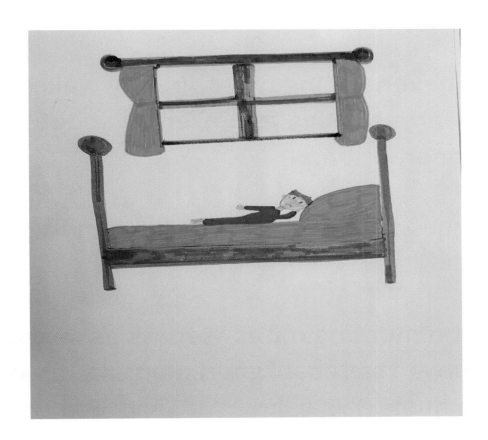

Tonight Johnny isn't allowed his hot chocolate before bed as punishment for his behaviour.

Johnny thinks this punishment is unfair and lies there imagining he has a Time

Machine that can take him back to earlier that day. When he goes back, he doesn't kick his truck in anger and he is much kinder to his mum.

Johnny soon falls to sleep.

The next morning when Johnny wakes up he seems to have forgotten all about his anger emotion.

He goes downstairs to the kitchen for breakfast.

"Good morning mum" he says as he sits down at the table "good morning Johnny" says mum.

Mum is happy that Johnny seems to be feeling happy this morning but mum is still feeling sad about yesterdays events.

At the breakfast table there is one extra pancake left over as Shannon didn't want hers. Johnny has decided that he wants this pancake, but Cecilia also wants it.

Johnny and Cecilia start to argue over who will get the last pancake and Johnnys anger emotion has been activated AGAIN!

Johnny jumps up and pushes Cecilia, Cecilia falls off her chair onto the floor and lands on her arm.

Cecilia starts to cry, her arm is hurting a lot and Mum must now take Cecilia to the hospital for an x ray to make sure nothing is broken.

Poor Cecilia.

Johnny is feeling terrible, he didn't mean to hurt Cecilia, he has allowed his angry emotion to control him again with dangerous and upsetting consequences.

Mum decides enough is enough! Johnny MUST learn to control his anger emotion.

First, Johnny must understand his anger and what is happening to his body when he feels angry.

Mum explains to Johnny and everyone else that anger is a natural response to something that upsets us. When we start to feel angry our bodies release a hormone which is called adrenaline. Adrenaline is super helpful if we are in a dangerous situation because it helps us to act quickly.

Adrenaline causes our muscles to become tighter and our hearts to beat faster. Blood is then sent to our arms and legs so we can fight or run very fast.

This is called our fight or flight response.

Johnny must start to recognise when this is happening to him and find ways to control it before it gets too far and he reacts in harmful ways.

Johnny has 3 sisters, Elsie May, Shannon and Cecilia, he also has a brother called Paul. Together they come up with a plan to help Johnny control his anger.

Mum asks Johnny to see if he can notice any changes he might feel in his body when he gets angry. Straight away he remembers squeezing his teeth tightly together, this is called a clenched jaw and is very common when someone is angry.

Johnny must look out for this sign and any others he might notice in his body next time he starts to feel angry and then he can try to find a way to stop himself from reacting in a way that's harmful to himself and others.

Noticing that you are becoming angry and finding a way to control how you react is a super power.

Mum tells Johnny a helpful way to satisfy his anger emotion "wrap your arms around yourself as if to give yourself a big hug and then squeeze tightly. This is a good method because you can do this anywhere.

Another good way to release adrenaline when you are angry is to jump up and down on a trampoline, but if you don't have a trampoline, running or jumping on the spot is also very effective.

Remember that controlling anger is not easy and you have to work hard and be strong.

Johnnys family get together a calming down kit...

This is a box with things inside to help him calm down if he is feeling frustrated or angry.

Inside the box is some squishy dough, squishing dough will help him release the anger he feels in his hands that causes him to make a tight fist. Squishy dough is also very fun!

Johnnys sister Elsie May has a great idea to put some bubble wrap inside the box too. Bubble wrap can be wrapped and twisted to pop lots of bubbles at once or they can be popped individually.

How do you like to pop bubble wrap?

Shannon comes up with the idea to put a pen and some paper in the box so if Johnny is thinking angry thoughts that might upset someone he can write them down and then screw up the paper and throw it in the bin. This means Johnny can get out his angry thoughts without hurting anyone's feelings.

Cecilia decides to add some colouring pens and colouring books to the box. Colouring can distract Johnny from his anger and give him enough time to think about a sensible way to react.

Can you think of anything else to add that might be helpful?

Johnnys brother Paul tells Johnny about a good way he gets out his anger, Paul goes to his room and screams or roars into his pillow.

Dad teaches Johnny some breathing exercises that he can do at home or anywhere else he might be, breathing calmly will help your body to calm down when you are feeling anxious or angry.

Dad teaches Johnny how to do these breathing exercises correctly.

Dad gets Johnny to lie down and place his soft tortoise on his Lower tummy .

When Johnny breathes in he should see the tortoise rise and when he breathes out the tortoise will come back down. Sometimes when we are angry or panic we take big breaths that can make our chest rise and this makes us feel uncomfortable, we need to take slow relaxing breaths that make our tummy rise and fall.

Johnny enjoys watching the tortoise rise and fall as he takes a slow breath in "1.2.3.4" and then a slow breath out "1.2.3.4"

After a few times practicing with his tortoise, Johnny is confident to do this standing up and without his tortoise.

Johnny is now prepared to try and take control of his anger emotion next time he starts to feel himself getting angry.

Later that day Johnny can't find his video game, he assumes his sister Shannon has taken it. He assumes this because sometimes she borrows it, but this time she insists she hasn't taken it.

Johnny doesn't believe Shannon and he is starting to feel angry, his jaw clenches tightly, he feels his heart beating fast and his face is feeling hot. It's very difficult but Johnny recognises and takes control of his anger emotion.
Johnny wraps his arms around himself and squeezes tightly. He then runs to his room and roars into his pillow. After this he takes some super breaths to calm down.

Johnny hasn't hurts anyone or broken anything and he hasn't upset anyone's feelings.

Johnny should be VERY proud of himself.

Now Johnny is calm and has time to think clearly he remembers he left his video game in the car when he went shopping with mum.

He apologises to Shannon for blaming her.

Learning to control anger is very difficult and accepting when you are wrong and apologising is a very brave and powerful thing to do.

 Next time you feel angry, try to notice what changes you feel in your body and maybe use some of the helpful methods Johnny and his family use to calm down.

Remember that YOU are in charge, not your anger emotion.

Johnny's exciting adventure with SANTA

It's Christmas Eve and Johnny is feeling very excited. He is ready for bed, but first he must leave out a cookie with milk for Santa and a carrot for the reindeer's so they can have a nibble when they arrive with presents.

Johnnys Mum and Dad tuck him up in bed.

" Night night Johnny, be sure to get some sleep" says Dad.
"Big day tomorrow" says mum "don't get up too early or you'll have no energy for your Christmas dinner"

Johnny tries and tries but he just can't sleep! He's just too excited about Santa visiting.

He squeezes his eyes shut tightly, but they just keep opening again.

He tries counting sheep jumping over a fence 1...2...3...4

It's no use, he just can't sleep.

Johnny is turning from side to side in his bed when all of a sudden he hears a jingle...

"Could this be Santa" he asks himself excitedly.

Johnny knows the rules, you must never try to catch Santa delivering presents or he might dash off without leaving any.
He closes his eyes, but then he hears someone say his name "Johnny"

Johnny quietly gets out of bed and peeps through the gap in his bedroom door, he sees a light coming from the living room and he notices the clock, it's midnight.

Johnny tip toes down the hall trying to be as quiet as a mouse, moving slowly towards the living room.

As Johnny reaches the living room, he sees Santa!

"Hello Johnny" says Santa "I've been waiting for you, you're one of the very few children chosen on Christmas Eve to come on a magical adventure and help me with my Christmas deliveries"

"A magical adventure!" Johnny asks excitedly. He can barely believe his eyes and ears.

As Johnny looks down at his feet, he is wearing Elf shoes! He then looks at his pyjamas which are now Elf clothes.
 "I'm dressed as an Elf" says Johnny.

"You're not dressed as and Elf, you are an Elf" replies Santa.

Santa goes on to explain that, every year children are recruited on Christmas Eve to help Santa with his Christmas deliveries and share in the magic.
"Christmas Elves" says Santa proudly.

"Wow" says Johnny "I'm a real elf"

With that, Santa says "come aboard the sleigh"
Suddenly by magic Johnny is on the sleigh.

On the sleigh are 7 other elves who were also recruited by Santa for his Christmas deliveries. Johnny pinches his leg to check he isn't dreaming.

Santa explains to Johnny that each elf will have a special connection to one reindeer for the evening.

Dasher, Dancer, Prancer, Vixen, Comet, Cupid, Donner, Blitzen and Rudolph. Rudolph is head reindeer who leads the sleigh.

"You will be connected to Prancer" says Santa.

Santa sits at the top of the sleigh and is always connected to Rudolph.

Johnny hears a deep cheery voice "hello Johnny, Prancer here" "I can hear Prancer says Johnny, this is so exciting"

"If you have any problems let me know and likewise for me" says Prancer.

"What sort of problems" asks Johnny.

"Well a few years ago" says Santa "all the reindeers would talk to me about all sorts of things on our Christmas Eve adventures, then one year Rudolph was hit by a shooting star which set him off course, the other reindeer's were unaware and carried on talking, I didn't hear Rudolph's cries, well let's just say it was a long night"

"Everyone ready?" Asks Santa "yes" all the Elves shout excitedly "then off we go"

The reindeer's fly off the roof, jingling all the way.

Johnny loves feeling the night air on his face, it's cool but at the same time he feels warm.

Santa stops at every house with children and leaves presents under the tree ready for when they wake up in the morning. Santa takes one elf and one reindeer with him each time. Santa gives the cookie to the elf, the reindeer eats the carrot and Santa drinks his milk.

Johnny gets to see so many sights on his journey, Westminster bridge and the London eye look amazing from the sky.

They fly over the Eiffel tower in France and the Empire State Building in America. It all looks so beautiful.

It's Johnnys turn to go into someone's house and help Santa place presents under the tree.

As Johnny places a present, he notices someone standing in the doorway, a little girl. Johnny remembers the rules "no peeping at Santa or no presents will be left"

Johnny tells the little girl to hurry back to bed before Santa sees her.

At that moment Johnny appears back on the sleigh.

"Next stop, the moon" says Santa

"The moon?" All the elves ask with wide eyes and curiosity in their voices.

"Yes" says Santa "we deliver gifts to those on the moon, Christmas is very special on the moon too"

"Who lives on the moon?" Asks Johnny

"You'll see" says Santa with a big smile on his face and a sparkle in his eyes "ho ho ho ho"

The reindeer's make their way up towards the moon.

They arrive on the moon! It's completely silent but then Santa moves towards a Crater… "we are going INSIDE the moon" says Santa.

Then by magic the ground inside the crater opens up!

Johnny can't believe his eyes when they get inside, there's bright colours, music and some very odd looking little creatures dancing around. They all seem very excited to see Santa

"These are the moon Dinkers " says Santa "the people who live inside our moon"

It's not like on Earth, everyone is asleep on Christmas Eve when Santa delivers

presents, but on the moon everyone is awake.

Santa gives each elf a sack of presents to hand out to all the little Dinkers.

As Johnny reaches into his sack he pulls out a ball of light for each little Dinker, they seem very excited for this bright gift.

One little Dinker gives Johnny a gift too, it looks like a little bouncy ball, except it's very bright like the gifts from Santa. This little ball of light makes Johnny feel very happy.

It's time to get back on the sleigh and go home.

The moon door opens up and they all get back on the sleigh, the little Dinker who gave Johnny his bright gift, gives him a hug goodbye.

Santa takes Johnny back home, he waves goodbye to the reindeer's and remaining elves and gives Santa a big hug!

"Thank you Johnny" says Santa " Ho Ho Ho" he says as the sleigh takes off.

"Thank you Santa for the best Christmas ever" Johnny whispers as the sleigh disappears.

Suddenly Johnny is back in his bedroom and is now wearing his pyjamas again. He gets into bed and falls fast to sleep.

As morning arrives, Johnny starts to wake up and he remembers it's CHRISTMAS!!

He runs out of his bedroom and wakes up Mum and Dad and his brothers and sisters. Everyone dashes to the living room to see the presents under the tree.

Johnny opens his presents, he has an Elf costume! He remembers his adventure and starts to tell everyone, but no one believes him.

"That sounds like a lovely dream" says Elsie May.

"It wasn't a dream was it?" He starts to wonder.

But then he feels something in his pocket, he reaches in and pulls it out. There it is, glowing brightly, his little ball of light!

As he looks closer, he sees some bright colours inside the ball.

"Little Dinkers" he whispers to himself.

MERRY CHRISTMAS!!!!

I hope you enjoyed reading Johnnys series.